EVERYDAY MYSTERIES

WHY DO LEAVES CHANGE COLORS?

By Marie Roesser

Gareth Stevens
PUBLISHING

Color Questions

When leaves start changing color, we know it's the season called fall or autumn. Do you ever wonder why leaves change colors? And why do they change to the colors that they do? Read on to learn the answers!

5

Chlorophyll Coloring

First, let's learn about leaves. Leaves are the part of a plant where the plant's food is made. Leaves have **pigments** in them that give them colors. A green leaf gets its color from a pigment called chlorophyll.

Plant Food

Chlorophyll absorbs, or takes in, **energy** from sunlight. The energy turns water and the gas called carbon dioxide into sugars. This is the plant's food. A gas called oxygen is **released** into the air. We need oxygen to live. This **process** is called photosynthesis.

PHOTOSYNTHESIS

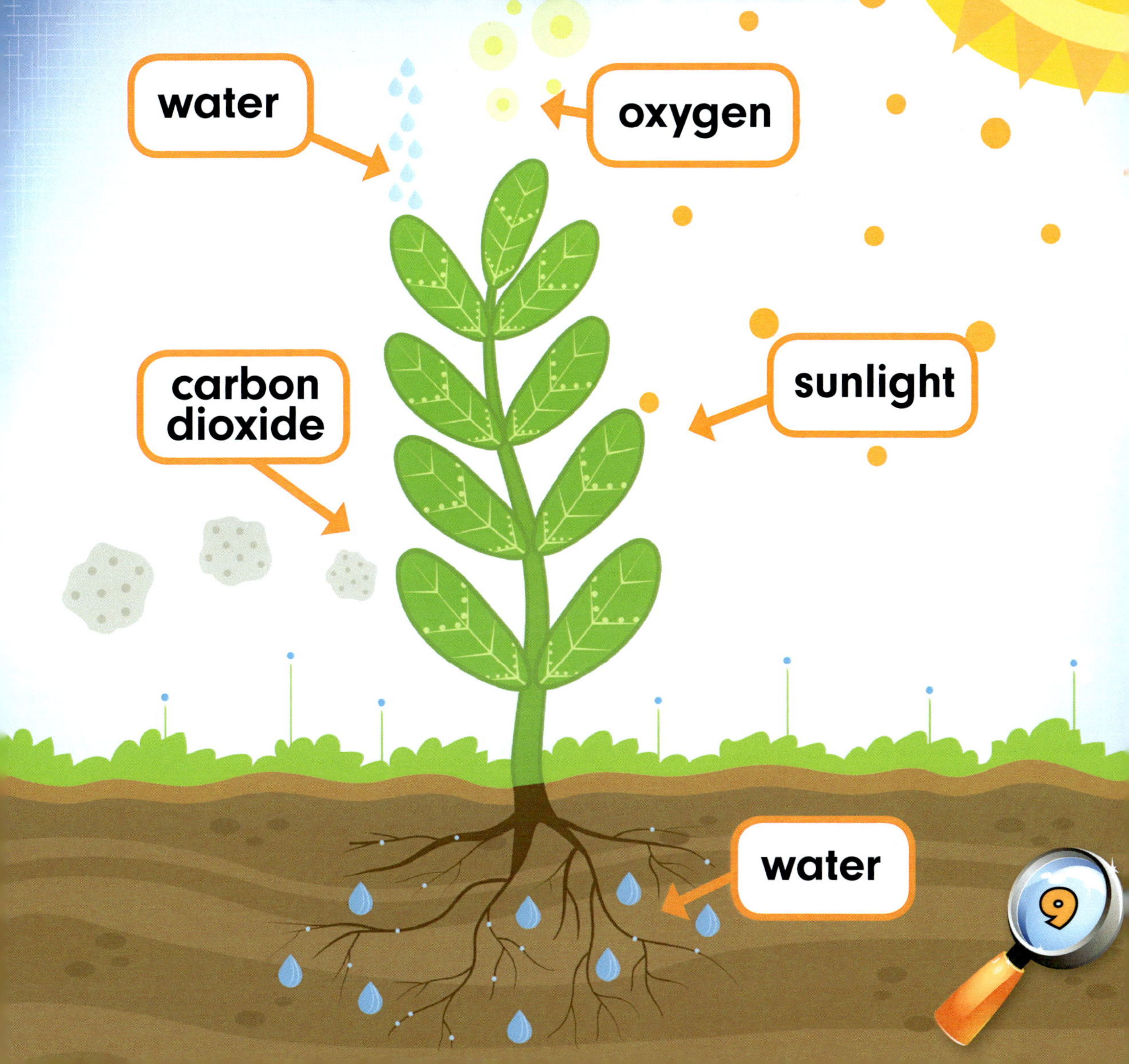

Losing Leaves

All trees lose their leaves. Some keep them for years. Some lose just a few at a time. However, some trees lose all their leaves for part of the year. These are called deciduous (dih-SIH-joo-wuhs) trees. Many kinds of oaks, maples, and elms are deciduous trees.

11

Goodbye, Green!

As summer ends, the days get shorter. The nights get longer. The weather becomes cooler too. Deciduous trees sense these changes. They make less chlorophyll because there's less sunlight for photosynthesis. They absorb their leaves' chlorophyll to save energy.

13

Hello, Yellow!

Carotenoids are a group of plant pigments found in the leaves of some trees. When chlorophyll disappears, leaves lose their green color. Carotenoids may be left. They turn leaves yellow, orange, or red. Carotenoids are also found in some vegetables—like carrots!

Anthocyanins are pigments that some trees make in the fall. They may help trees absorb leaves' **nutrients**. Anthocyanins can look red or purple. When leaves begin to die, pigments called tannins turn them brown. Leaf pigments can mix to color leaves too.

Letting Go

In the fall, a leaf may grow a special **layer** of cells where it's fixed to its tree. This layer is not as strong. It allows the leaf to fall off the tree easily. Some trees keep their leaves until new ones grow.

Watch the Weather

Weather **conditions** can affect leaves. Lack of rain can slow or speed up changing leaf colors. Leaves may fall early too. A strong **frost** can kill leaves. Do leaves change color where you live? Many people travel far to see beautiful leaf colors!

HOW LEAVES CHANGE COLORS

1 Trees produce chlorophyll. This gives leaves a green color.

2 When the days get shorter, deciduous trees make less chlorophyll. They absorb their leaves' chlorophyll.

3 The colors of other pigments show in leaves.

4 When leaves start to die, they turn brown.

GLOSSARY

condition: the state in which something lives

energy: power used to do something, such as grow or work

frost: a thin layer of ice that forms on the ground or on plants because of cold air

layer: one thickness of something lying over or under another

nutrient: something a living thing needs to grow and stay alive

pigment: a substance that gives a plant or animal color

process: a series of steps or actions taken to complete something

release: to set something free or to let go of something

FOR MORE INFORMATION

BOOKS

Bishop, Celeste. *Why Do Plants Have Leaves?* New York, NY: PowerKids Press, 2016.

Brennan, Linda Crotta. *Leaves Change Color.* Ann Arbor, MI: Cherry Lake Publishing, 2015.

Reinke, Beth Bence. *Why Do Leaves Change Color?* Mankato, MN: Child's World, 2016.

WEBSITES

Why Do Leaves Change Color?
scijinks.gov/leaves-color/
Check out more about the answer to this question here.

Why Do Leaves Change Color?
eekwi.org/veg/trees/treestruecolor.htm
Learn more about leaf color and weather.

Publisher's note to educators and parents: Our editors have carefully reviewed these websites to ensure that they are suitable for students. Many websites change frequently, however, and we cannot guarantee that a site's future contents will continue to meet our high standards of quality and educational value. Be advised that students should be closely supervised whenever they access the internet.

INDEX